FRESH OUT

MICHAEL KINGSWOOD

Contents

About This Book

Newly released after fifteen years in prison, Bill seeks to restart his life, and get revenge on the woman who framed him.

Fresh Out is a 5,600 word short crime story.

Enjoy the book! After you're done, please come to Michael's website and sign up for his mailing list at michaelkingswood.com/newsletter-signup/. Guaranteed to be spam free, he uses it to announce new releases and special promotions for his fans.

Fresh Out

B ill couldn't get used to how his clothes felt. After fifteen years of wearing nothing but prison coveralls, the jeans and red, long-sleeved collard shirt he had on when he was booked seemed like someone's else's attire.

And here, sitting in the passenger seat of Joey's car, he kept expecting to hear a guard shouting his name, ripping him a new one for not being dressed right.

He watched the streetlights that lined the highway leading down toward Norfolk pass on either side, and could not shake that feeling. Or the little panicky feeling that threatened to jump up through his chest at the expansive world out there, a world without walls or fences that he was now able to experience, once again.

Inside, he'd scoffed at guys who talked about people they knew who couldn't hack it out in the world and who had gotten busted just so they could come back to the clink, to the world they knew and understood. What kind of moronic pussy would do something like that?

But now, looking out at it for the first time in so long, Bill understood.

"Feels good, don't it."

From behind the wheel, Joey looked over at Bill and grinned. He was Bill's age, mid-40s, with curly black hair that was flecked with grey strands here and there, dark eyes, and a handsome oval face and ready grin that always attracted the ladies. He had done well for himself while Bill was inside, to all appearances. He drove a Dodge Charger with all the trimmings, and wore a stylish black leather jacket over a white shirt that Bill was pretty sure was silk. He was surrounded by the subtle musk of expensive cologne, and his watch glittered silver; probably cost a few grand. If that weren't enough, he'd had his left incisor capped with gold.

Doing ok.

Bill shrugged, and Joey chuckled.

"It takes a little getting used to. I wasn't in as long as you, but I know. Believe me."

Joey had done three years for dealing, back before he got smart about things. He was mostly straight now, or at least had been back before Bill went away. Pretty much the exact opposite route Bill had taken, come to think on it.

But then, Joey had actually done what he was put away for.

Bill couldn't relate to that.

They turned off at the exit to Hampton, and Bill raised an eyebrow Joey's way. "You don't live in Chesapeake anymore?"

Joey shrugged as he eased the car into its new lane. "After Lisa left, I - " He broke off when he saw Bill's expression. "Shit. Sorry, forgot you didn't know." He sighed and shook his head. "She kicked me to the curb two years ago. Got it in her head that she's destined to be a movie star. Took Kevin, and split to LA."

"No shit?"

Joey shrugged again. "Chicks, man. What're you gonna do?"

Which was one thing, but Lisa had taken Joey's son with her. If a girl had done that to Bill…

But then, Rachel had done that to him, hadn't she? Worse, actually. She'd set it up so he would take the fall for her caper, and then he went to rot in prison where he hadn't seen his son in fifteen years. While she was probably living the high life and banging quarterbacks, or something.

He was going to need dental surgery if he didn't stop grinding his teeth. He focused back on Joey. "Sorry, man."

Joey grinned at him. "Not your fault, brother."

He turned left, and they departed the main road for a quieter residential street. It was one of those streets where the trees planted on either side reached out and covered the road with their branches, with houses that were not McMansions but still respectably big and constructed with that distinctly southern front porch that's begging for a swing where a father could sit to clean his shotgun while his daughter was off on her first date.

Halfway down the block, Joey turned left into the driveway of a single-story house that, of course, had the required porch. A pair of lamps that flickered like torches lit the stairs leading up to the porch and the front door. The place was lit as though occupied already.

He looked sidelong at Joey. "You're not throwing me a party, are you?"

Joey sniffed and shut off the engine. "Nothing major," he said, and grinned at him.

Bill followed Joey up the stairs to his house and could not shake off a sense of trepidation. The absolute last thing he wanted to do right now was deal with people. Really, he just wanted to get settled, have a beer, then hit the rack. He had a lot to do, and the sooner he got about it, the better.

Bill's house was spacious, but not enormous. The door opened into a great room that spanned most of the house's width. Deep blue paint on the walls balanced the off-white tiles that made up the flooring. A simply elegant dining set with seating for six lay off to the right. Directly in front of the door, a black leather sectional couch faced a flat screen that was wider than Bill was tall. The kitchen was in the rear right portion of the room, with white cabinets and a dark grey stone countertop bar splitting the appliances from the living and dining areas. Two closed doors stood off to Bill's left, and a hallway just to the right of the flat screen lead back deeper into the house. Muted jazz was playing as they walked in, and the place had a pleasant almost pinewood odor.

"Home sweet home," Joey said, spreading his hands to take in the space and grinning broadly. "You're in there," he pointed toward the second of the two doors to the left. "Got your own bathroom." He gestured toward the hallway. "I'm in back. Put your stuff down and get settled; I'll get you a drink."

That sounded real good, actually.

Bill went through the indicated door and found a decently sized bedroom with beige walls and the same white tile floor. A queen-sized bed with blue sheets stood against the far wall, atop a thick blue throw rug that expanded out most of the way over the room's floor. Better for bare feet that way. Two doors were on the rear wall, one ajar leading into the bathroom. The other was a closet, Bill presumed. A darkly-stained hardwood dresser standing against the wall opposite the bed completed the room's ensemble.

Not too bad.

Bill dropped the plastic bag containing the belongings that the prison had released back to him onto the bed and stepped into the bathroom. When he'd finished his business, he went back into the great room.

Joey was not alone. He stood in the entryway to the house not far from Bill's room, and he was flanked by a pair of utter hotties.

They both wore skin-tight black evening gowns that came to mid-thigh, diamonds in their ears, and gold necklaces on their throats. The one of the Joey's left was the taller of the two, and blonde, with flowing hair that fell well past her shoulders, smoldering green eyes, and the kind of tight body you'd expect from a dancer. To Joey's right was a brunette, with pixie cut hair. She was more curvy —Joey estimated a D cup—without being fat, and carried a trio of champagne flutes in one hand and an un-opened bottle of Dom in the other. They both smiled warmly at him when he emerged.

Joey was grinning ear to ear. "Bill. Meet Tami," he touched the blonde's shoulder, then the brunette's, "and Ricki."

It was all Bill could do to manage a surprised, "Hi."

The girls looked at each other, then Ricki stepped forward. She walked slowly, seductively, past him, heading toward the guest room. "Hi Bill," she said as she reached his shoulder, "we're your freedom party."

Bill swallowed, following her with his eyes. A light touch on his shoulder brought his attention around to Tami, who was tracing her fingertips down his arm until they reached his elbow. Then she slipped her arm into his and began gently turning him toward the guest room door. "Come on, handsome," she said in a smoky voice, and Bill's knees almost buckled.

It had been a long, long, long, long, *long* time. Really damn long.

He didn't even think about not going with them.

Just before he stepped back into the guest room, he looked back and saw Joey still standing there with that shit eating grin.

"Welcome back to the world, buddy," Joey said.

BILL FOUND Joey the next morning sitting at his kitchen counter, dressed in a blue bathrobe and drinking a cup of coffee. As he walked up, dressed in only his boxer briefs, Joey looked him over and raised an eyebrow, then shrugged.

"Coffee's in the machine," he said.

Bill walked around the counter and fished around in the cabinets for a bit until he found Joey's stash of coffee mugs, then he poured himself a cup.

It was good. Anything was, compared with the swill they served in the clink. But still, this was outstanding. He swirled the coffee in his mouth, savoring the flavor, then swallowed and raised an eyebrow Joey's way.

Joey chuckled. "Good shit, eh?"

Bill nodded. He leaned onto the counter, across from Joey, and rested his elbows on the countertop. "Thanks for last night."

Joey grinned lasciviously. "I'd say it's my pleasure but it's more yours, right?" He glanced sidelong at the clock mounted the adjacent wall. It was almost 7:30. "Girls haven't taken off yet, have they?"

Bill shook his head.

"Good. I paid for the whole night until 9 this morning. And multiple shots on goal." Joey looked back at Bill and his grin twisted into a smirk. "If I were you I'd make sure to get another nut or two from each of them before they leave."

Bill nodded slowly. He'd take that under advisement. But enticing as that idea was, he had more pressing matters on his mind. "So. Rachel and Jason."

Joey's smirk faded into a businesslike expression. He looked down at the mug in his hands and sighed. "Yeah. Well, Jason split town right after High School. Bounced around a bit, but I hear he's up in Philly now." He looked back up, meeting Bill's eyes again, clearly reluctant to go any further.

"And Rachel?"

"You can't let it go, man? I know how you feel, but - "

Bill growled to cut Joey off, and found he was clenching his mug so hard his hand was shaking. He shoved his chin out, fixing Joey with his "Mess With Me And Die" prison yard stare. "You don't fucking know how I feel." He drew a deep breath, and releasing his mug, stabbed the air between himself and Joey with his index finger. "Fifteen years! That bitch stole fifteen years of my life. Fifteen years without my son - !"

Joey recoiled in alarm, and Bill realized he was shouting. He stopped.

Joey raised his hands, palms out toward Bill, and spoke slowly. "I mean I understand, ok?" He paused, then when Bill did not respond said again, "Ok?"

Bill took a breath to get control of himself, then nodded. "Yeah. Sorry."

"Look man, all I'm saying is you just got *out* of

the clink. Why do you want to do something to get yourself thrown back in? You gone all institutional on me?"

Bill paused at the paralleling of his thoughts from the previous night. Was he just angling for a way to get back to the place that, terrible as it was, had become familiar, almost home?

He shook his head. "I can't let it go, brother."

Joey looked him in the eye for a long several seconds then, with a sigh, nodded. "Ok. Rachel's still in town, down in the 'hood. She's not doing so well, what I hear. I got her address from a guy I know. You can…well…" He left the rest unsaid.

Bill nodded his thanks. "You got my stuff?"

"Yeah." Joey pushed himself back from the counter and straightened. "One sec." He turned and left the kitchen, heading toward the hallway leading to his bedroom. A few minutes later, he came back with a black duffle bag that was stuffed to the gills. He set the bag down on the counter and slid it toward Bill. "Here you go."

Bill unzipped the bag and opened it. Here were all the rest of his worldly possessions. A couple pairs of pants, some shirts, and boxers. His copy of Crime And Punishment and his baseball card collection. His DD-214. A few other nicknacks and books. And there, at the bottom of the bag, a stainless steel revolver with a black grip and a box of .357 Magnum rounds. The serial numbers had been acid-etched away long before Bill went to the clink, and it had been his favorite gun for a long, long time.

He was ready for business.

"Thanks, man." He zipped up the duffle bag and downed the last of his coffee. Then he picked up the bag and headed back toward the guest room.

Joey had a point about the girls, after all.

BILL COULD TELL it was Rachel weaving down the sidewalk from half a block away. It was something about the way she held herself, the way she moved. Even after all these years, and a whole lot of booze, drugs, or both tonight, that distinctive sway of her hips had not gone away.

He sat behind the wheel of Joey's car, across the street and a building over from her apartment complex. Although that was doing the dilapidated, gang-sign tagged heap of bricks where she lived more credit than it was due. The place looked like it should have been condemned before Bill went away, and hadn't been kept up since then.

And he thought the cell block had looked depressing.

It was late. Almost 1 in the morning, and most of the street traffic had died away. Only the occasional car came driving past, moving quickly down the lines of parallel-parked cars that flanked the street's two lanes so as to get through this neighborhood as quickly as possible. And the last group of pedestrians had swaggered past, hooping and hollering at each other in drunken revelry, about ten minutes ago.

It was just her, making her slow, meandering progress from the illumination of one street light to the next as she approached her building, and him.

She had on a black trench coat, though it had not been raining, and had her strawberry blond—probably going to grey now like Bill's was—hair pulled back in a ponytail that didn't quite touch the coat's collar. Looked like pumps on her feet, though he couldn't make out the color. Very nearly stripper heels.

Bill ran his hand beneath the leather jacket he was wearing and traced his fingertips along the grip of his revolver, tucked into his belt on his right hip, and could not keep an anticipatory smile from his lips.

He got out of the car and closed the door gently, so as to not make a lot of noise, then set off up the street in the direction she was coming from. His plan was to pass her, then loop around and follow her back to her building.

But he needn't have bothered. She never looked in his direction, and the way she kept staggering from one side of the sidewalk to the other he wondered if she really noticed anything at all.

Another car sped past in his direction, illuminating her face for a second before it continued on its way. Sure enough she had her eyes fixed firmly on the sidewalk in front of her. Oblivious.

Bill went ahead and crossed the street as soon as he was past her, and stopped behind a late-model mustang that had somehow not been keyed, tagged, or had its tires slashed. She was near to the entrance to her building now, and had stopped to fish around in her purse for something, probably her keys.

A few seconds later, she staggered forward again, all but falling into the door. It took a good thirty seconds for her to fumble with the keys before she found the right one and let herself in.

Bill was moving before she finished stepping through the door, hurrying to get there before the door swung shut; he didn't have the key and he hadn't tried to pick a lock in sixteen years.

He just made it, sticking his hand into the gap between the door and its frame with only a couple inches to go. He paused there and peeked in before opening it further.

Rachel had proceeded onward without a backward glance. He caught a glimpse of her turning right around a corner ahead before she passed out of sight.

He followed.

The interior of the building was as unappealing as the exterior. The carpet used to be burgundy but was holed in so many places, and stained in so many others, that it could not claim that honor any more. The yellowish paint on the walls was peeling, and there were noticeable cracks in the crown molding. Several of the cracks ran straight across the ceiling, and there were a bunch of water stains there as well.

Rachel sure was keeping herself in style.

Bill peeked around the corner, and saw her stopped in front of an apartment about halfway down the adjoining hall, on the left. Again she was fumbling with her keys; she dropped them this time before she was able to get them sorted out. A moment later she was inside, and he set out down the hall toward her door.

He expected he would have to knock, but when he reached her apartment, number seven, he found the door a couple inches ajar.

So much the easier.

He pushed the door open and stepped through. And stopped.

Rachel's apartment was in even worse condition than the building. There was a hole in the wall to the right of the door, where a coat hook might have been at some point. To the left, her tiny kitchen was covered in grime like it hadn't been cleaned in a month. Dirty pans were piled in the sink, and the counter was littered with empty bottles of cheap beer or liquor of all varieties. A bong, with the charred nub from the last joint to be smoked in it, stood prominently in a place of honor near the front.

The living room, directly ahead, had a sagging old beige sofa directly across from the door and beneath a single long window that spanned the length of the room. The curtains, once white but now grey from dirt and years of smoke, were closed, blocking the view of a brick wall unless Bill missed his guess. In front of the sofa stood a coffee table that might had been stained red-brown at one point but was now so scratched and covered in cigarette burns it didn't matter. An old-school TV—as in, the kind that was in existence before Bill went away—sat against the wall to the left, a yellow folding chair sitting directly in front of it.

The entire place smelled of cigarette and marijuana smoke, despite the pathetic attempts of a plug-in air freshener in a wall outlet beneath the hole in the wall.

Rachel stood with her back to the door in front of the coffee table, messing with her earrings.

Bill just looked at her for a long couple of seconds.

She was thin. Much thinner than the lushly-curved woman who had used to be his wife. Her hair was greying, but it had thinned also. Age had caught up to her as well, it seemed. Well, it wouldn't do any more catching after tonight.

Bill drew the revolver and let it hang in his hand by his right thigh, then he kicked the door shut with his heel. It made a loud THUNK as it shut, and Rachel jumped.

She spun around, her eyes widening in alarm. "What the fuck do you think you're - "

Bill interrupted her. "Hello, Rachel."

She narrowed her eyes, but no recognition appeared on her face. He took a step toward her and smiled thinly. "Don't recognize me?"

He knew he had changed during his time in the clink. His hairline had receded, and he had developed frown lines around his mouth and eyes. He'd also lost a lot of body fat; all that great prison food. But he was still the man he had been when they were together all those years ago.

Of course, had he not known who she was he might not have placed her as his former wife, turned betrayer.

She looked like hell. Her face had always been narrow; now it was gaunt, to match the excessive skinniness of the rest of her frame. Her eyes were sunken pits, with dark shadows beneath them that looked permanent. Her skin was pockmarked, and her hair was thin, brittle-looking. She wasn't wrinkled like he was so much as withered, and there was a wildness about her that belied that complete lack of life or soul in her eyes.

Part of him cringed to look at her.

It took a few seconds for it to register with her, then she nodded. "So you got out, huh? Good for you. Not sure what - "

"Where's the money, Rachel?"

He moved another step closer. She half-snorted, half spat and spread her hands out, but she didn't reply.

"You and Ronnie stole half a million dollars, and pinned it on me." Another step.

She shook her head and let out a bitter almost-laugh. "There is no money, Bill. Ronnie took it and ran off six months after you went in. This," she swept her hand around the pit of an apartment, "is all I got." She made a drunkenly exaggerated "go away" wave with her left hand in his general direction.

And Ronnie was in the clink now, or so Bill had been told, and wouldn't be getting out while he was still vertical. Bill had expected Ronnie would screw her over, but he still couldn't wrap his head around how Rachel could have been so stupid as to trust a guy like him.

Then again, it really was more like she had come to hate Bill, and wanted to get back at him over that girl in Kansas City. And she hadn't cared about how, or with whom.

He sighed and looked down at the floor before his feet. He'd long since come to terms with the part he had played in his own demise. If he hadn't cheated...

It didn't excuse what she did. Nothing could.

Still...

"You ever hear from our son?" He looked back up at her face in time to see her grimace, as though the very idea was distasteful to her.

"Nah, he's out in Vegas or something." Vegas. Of course she wouldn't know where Jason was. "Don't want nothing to do with - " Her words cut off as she finally looked at him fully. And saw the gun.

She swallowed, hard. "You here to kill me, that it?" She sounded decidedly neutral about the entire concept.

Bill did not answer.

A second passed, and a change came over her. She adjusted her balance so that her right hip stuck out in that pose she used to use that was so damn sexy, and a slow smile appeared on her face. Problem was, on her overly thin frame the pose seemed stilted, and the smile that was supposed to be seductive was sick, twisted.

"Or maybe you want to get it on, for old time's sake?" She tugged at the belt on her trench coat. The knot that had been holding the coat loosened, and the coat slid off her shoulders onto the floor.

She was nude beneath it.

Bill had cringed before upon seeing her face. The rest of her… She must have been coming back from a trick, but who would pay for *that*?

The woman he had known and loved, the lushly curved and sensuous soul who had so completely turned him on before, was gone.

The breasts that she used to love smothering him with were no more. They flopped down her torso like water balloons that had been drained of fluid leaving only the rubber behind, and part of her left nipple was gone, like it had been ripped away. Or bitten off. The bones of her hips stuck out through her skin, and her ribs showed through. Her skin seemed to hang off her, and stretch marks that their son had not caused before Bill went away rippled across her belly. The pockmarks that blemished her face continued everywhere else on her body, and scabs further desecrated her skin. Her pubic hair was as thin and ratty as that atop her head, and he thought he saw a scab or two there also.

Track marks were clearly visible on her arms… and was that another one on her inner thigh?

He found himself retreating, and she advanced on him in a slow, hip-rolling gait that was probably supposed to be sexy but just came off as an obscene perversion of beauty.

"How about it, Bill?" She had closed the distance between them without him realizing it. She traced a finger down his chest to his belly before alighting on the top of his belt. This close, the smell of her sweat overwhelmed the faint straw-berry perfume she was wearing.

She licked her cracked lips, and the sight made him raise the gun instinctively.

Rachel met the gun with her left hand, and drew her fingers sensually down its length.

"Come on, baby," she sank down to her knees in front of him, and guided the gun forward so it filled the space between them. "You remember how good it was."

She bent forward and kissed the gun's muzzle. She turned her head to his right and moved down the barrel towards his hand, kissing the cold metal the entire way. Then her tongue flicked out, and she ran it back up the barrel, then across the muzzle and down the other side.

Bill squirmed as memories flooded into him, how she used to do that to him, and how good she made it.

She looked up and met his eyes with hers as her tongue finished running down the left side of the barrel, and she gave his thumb a light kiss.

Cold, dead eyes that showed no joy, no sensual-ity, no feeling of any kind. Eyes without a soul be-hind them.

Whatever arousal Bill had been feeling from the memories of their previous time together fled beneath the reality of the…thing…kneeling before him. At least the hookers Joey had bought for him were good actresses: they had made it seem as though they really enjoyed what they were doing with him, that it had brought them some pleasure above and beyond the money they had received.

In fairness, they had actually seemed to really enjoy being *together*, but that was not relevant just then.

There was not even a facsimile of desire or

pleasure in the gaze of the creature before him—Bill could not bear to give it the name that his former love used, once upon a time. Only emptiness and resignation over an act to be performed, and beneath it an all-consuming and insatiable need, looked up at him.

Reflexively, he cocked the hammer of the revolver back.

Rachel froze, her eyes locked on his. "No?" She let out a breath and her shoulders sagged, then she nodded, ever so slightly. "Fine." She placed both hands around the barrel—the same way she used to grip him, back in the day—but instead of guiding it to her mouth, she moved the muzzle dead center on her forehead.

"Do it."

She stared up at him, and he met her gaze. A tear formed in the corner of her right eye and flowed down her cheek.

"Go on." Her voice was becoming more insistent.

His index finger moved inside the trigger guard and rested on the trigger. Then he paused, just looking at her.

"DO IT!" She was shouting now, but it wasn't anger or fear behind that shout.

He saw it in her dead, soulless eyes.

She was living in her own private little hell, her every day a misery of despair and hopelessness. Every man preyed upon her, every woman competed against or belittled her. There was no solace, no rest, except for the needle…and that would not do for long.

Rachel's daily existence was a punishment far greater than any he could ever dream to dole out. The bullet would be a release, a mercy. And from the faint glimmer of hope in her eyes he saw she knew it, just as she knew she would never have the courage to do it herself.

No.

Bill lowered the hammer and stepped back, pulling the revolver out of her hands.

Rachel lost her balance and fell, face-first, to the floor, only catching herself on her elbows at the last second. She looked up at him, and that glimmer of hope faded, leaving only empty despair.

"Goodbye, Rachel." Bill turned away from her and tucked the revolver back into his belt, then moved toward the door.

She was silent until he had the door open, then -

"You dickless bastard! Get back here! You spineless little pussy! You - "

He let the invectives, the insults, the obscenity wash over him as he left her apartment. He knew it was not him she was screaming at.

Halfway down the hall, her shouts turned into an incoherent scream of primal fury.

By the time he reached the outer door, fury had given way to soul-destroying despair, and her scream had turned into a series of sobbing wails.

Six months of working the sorry-ass job his PO got for him. Six months of crashing in Joey's spare room and keeping his nose meticulously clean. Six months of not going out, and saving every penny he got. And finally, Bill obtained permission to leave the state.

He bought a jalopy and drove the five hours up the Delmarva peninsula to Philly, to one particular neighborhood.

The Web had existed before he went away, but everything was easier now, more connected. It hadn't been hard to find out where to go.

He sat in his car, looking at the apartment complex where Jason lived, and realized he was afraid. More afraid than he had been on his first day in the clink. More afraid than when he had asked Rachel, heart in his hand, to marry him. More afraid than when he'd made his first jump in Airborne training.

It had been so long. The boy he knew was gone. Jason was a man of twenty-two now, and probably full of anger with the father who had left him behind, so many years ago, to go to prison.

This was stupid. He wouldn't want to see Bill, let alone talk with him. Better to just head back to Hampton now, save himself the heartache and embarrassment.

Instead of starting the car and driving away, Bill opened the door and got out. He squared his shoulders and marched across the street through a gap in the traffic, and into the apartment complex.

The complex was one of those horseshoe-shaped arrangements, with an opening to the outside world at one end, a playground and swimming pool in the center, and two levels of apartments in the ring around the pool. The courtyard was planted with bushes and flowers around the pool, and a couple of elms back by the playground, giving the entire place a homey, relaxing feel. The swimming pool was empty, but a couple of moms sat on a bench by the playground and watched as a half dozen kids screamed and ran around on the playground.

Nice place.

The manager's office was on Bill's left as he

walked into the courtyard, but he paid it no mind. He knew where he was going.

A set of black painted, wrought-iron stairs to his right led up to the second level. He ascended the stairs, paying little heed to the ominous creak they gave as he placed his weight onto the second-to-last step. Then he was on the second level, and he looked around.

The door closest to him read 232 on a brass label plate beneath the dirt-brown door's peephole.

Bill pulled a folded up sheet of paper out of his pocket and checked it. Jason was apartment 217. Probably about halfway around.

He set out, and sure enough almost exactly on the opposite side of the ring from that first place, he stopped in front of the door labelled 217.

There was a mat set out in front of the door, the cheery "Welcome" ringed by creeping green vines from which bloomed purple and pink flowers.

Bill stepped onto the mat and faced the door, and the peephole seemed to stare at him. Through him.

Doubt, fear, and excitement battled in his chest, but doubt most of all. Did he really think Jason wanted to see him? And even if he did, did Bill really have the right to impose on him now, before he really had himself together?

Again the impulse to turn around and head back to Hampton reared up inside him.

Instead, Bill drew a deep breath, squared his shoulders, and knocked on the door.

Thank you for reading my book. I hope you enjoyed reading it as much as I enjoyed writing it.

Every review helps an author out, so whether you loved this book, hated it, or something in between, please take a minute to tell other readers what you thought. All of the online retailers make it very easy to do, and I would really appreciate it.

Feel free to come say hi at my website or on Facebook. I always enjoy hearing from readers, especially since you all are, collectively, my boss.

I also have a weekly podcast, Story Time With Michael Kingswood, where I read stories and talk through some of the latest goings on in my world. I'd love to see you there.

Thanks again. My best to you and yours.

Warm Regards,
Michael Kingswood

Mailing List

If you enjoyed this book and would like word on new releases and special deals from Michael Kingswood, sign up for his newsletter on his website. Guaranteed to be spam-free, you can opt out at any time. And you can rest assured he will not share your information with anyone, for any reason.

https://michaelkingswood.com/newsletter-signup/

About The Author

Michael Kingswood is 20-year veteran of the US Navy submarine force and a lifelong fan of science fiction and fantasy literature. His work has appeared in numerous collections and anthologies, to include the Fiction River Anthology series from WMG publishing. He holds a bachelors degree in Mechanical Engineering as well as a Master of Engineering Management and a Master of Business Administration. He has four children and currently resides in San Diego.

Find Michael Kingswood online at:

www.michaelkingswood.com

www.facebook.com/michael.kingswood

steemit.com/@michaelkingswood

More Books By Michael Kingswood

Glimmer Vale Chronicles

Glimmer Vale

Out-Dweller

Tollard's Peak

Robbed Blind

Wedding Gifts: A Glimmer Vale Chronicles Story

The Falconer's Stairs

Glimmer Vale Omnibus Edition #1

The Pericles Conspiracy

Passing In The Night

The Pericles Conspiracy

Dawn Of Enlightenment

Masters Of The Sun

Novellas

What Lurks Between

The Necromancer's Lair

The Champion

Veritas Morte

Story Collections

Tales Of Adventure #1

Tales Of Adventure #2

Short Story 10-Pack

A Jar Of Mixed Treats

Short Mystery 10-Pack

Short Fiction

Michael has also published a number of shorter works,
links to which can be found on his website.

www.ingramcontent.com/pod-product-compliance
Lightning Source LLC
Chambersburg PA
CBHW032054180726
48284CB00004B/1328